Samuel French Acting Edition

AF278448

The Oregon Trail

by Bekah Brunstetter

||SAMUEL FRENCH||

FOR PRODUCTION INQUIRIES

UNITED STATES AND CANADA
info@concordtheatricals.com
1-866-979-0447

UNITED KINGDOM AND EUROPE
licensing@concordtheatricals.co.uk
020-7054-7200

Each title is subject to availability from Concord Theatricals Corp.,
depending upon country of performance. Please be aware that THE
OREGON TRAIL may not be licensed by Concord Theatricals Corp. in
your territory. Professional and amateur producers should contact the
nearest Concord Theatricals Corp. office or licensing partner to verify
availability.

This work is published by Samuel French, an imprint of Concord
Theatricals Corp.

MUSIC AND THIRD PARTY MATERIALS USE NOTE

Licensees are solely responsible for obtaining formal written permission from copyright owners to use copyrighted music and/or other copyrighted third-party materials (e.g., artworks, logos) in the performance of this play and are strongly cautioned to do so. If no such permission is obtained by the licensee, then the licensee must use only original music and materials that the licensee owns and controls. Licensees are solely responsible and liable for clearances of all third-party copyrighted materials, including without limitation music, and shall indemnify the copyright owners of the play(s) and their licensing agent, Concord Theatricals Corp., against any costs, expenses, losses and liabilities arising from the use of such copyrighted third-party materials by licensees. For music, please contact the appropriate music licensing authority in your territory for the rights to any incidental music.

IMPORTANT BILLING AND CREDIT REQUIREMENTS

If you have obtained performance rights to this title, please refer to your licensing agreement for important billing and credit requirements.

THE OREGON TRAIL was first produced by the Fault Line Theatre (Aaron Rossini and Craig Wesley Divino, Co-Artistic Directors) at the WP Theater in New York on January 22, 2017. The performance was directed by Geordie Broadwater, with set design by Tristan Jeffers, costume design by Izzy Fields, lighting design by John Eckert, and sound design by Chad Raines. The stage manager was Shayna O'Neill. The cast was as follows:

JANE	Liba Vaynberg
MARY ANNE	Laura Ramadei
BILLY	Juan Arturo
THEN JANE	Emily Louise Perkins
CLANCY	Jimmy King
GAME	Craig Wesley Divino

THE OREGON TRAIL was subsequently produced by Flying V at the Writer's Center in Maryland from September 3-20, 2017. The performance was directed by Amber McGinnis, with set and costume design by Kathryn Kawecki, lighting design by Kristin A. Thompson, and sound design by Neil McFadden. The stage manager was Allie Heiman. The cast was as follows:

JANE	Madeline Key
MARY ANNE	Julia Klavans
BILLY	Will Hayes
THEN JANE	Kelsey Meiklejohn
CLANCY	Ryan Tumulty
GAME	Zachary Fernebok

CHARACTERS

Present

JANE – a contemporary young woman, prone to overthinking things

MARY ANNE – Jane's controlling sister, always upbeat

BILLY – the hottest prepubescent guy in school

GAME – the omnipotent voice of The Oregon Trail, a voice-over or a live actor

1848

THEN JANE – a young girl traversing the country with her family via the Oregon Trail

MARY ANNE – her seemingly perfect sister (played by contemporary Mary Anne)

CLANCY – their father

MATT – the proprietor of a general store (doubled with Billy or Game, if played by a live actor)

NOTE ON GAME MUSIC

A license to produce *The Oregon Trail* does not include a performance license for any game music from the The Oregon Trail computer game. The publisher and author suggest that the licensee contact ASCAP or BMI to ascertain the music publisher and contact such music publisher to license or acquire permission for performance of the game music. If a license or permission is unattainable for the game music, the licensee may not use that music in *The Oregon Trail* but should create an original composition in a similar style or use a similar song in the public domain. For further information, please see Music Use Note on page 3.

PART I

GAME. GOING BACK TO 1997.

> *A computer lab at a nice private K-12, where privileged kids go.*
>
> *A wall clock's hands read 3:27 p.m. It's that weird time after school when you're there for rehearsal, or practice, or you're just – weird.*
>
> **JANE**, *thirteen, who is growing into her body in a bad way, sits at a desk on her sweet-ass giant Nokia cell phone. She is insecure, scared, alone, but has a sweet weirdness to her. Her brain is big in her head, her heart bigger in her chest. She is calling someone for the tenth time who is just not picking up. She leaves a message.*

JANE. Mom. MOM. MOMMMMM. Are you home? MOM PICK UP. Please?! You were supposed to be here an hour ago. Mary Anne's got violin and I'm still here and everyone was looking at me like a forgotten person so I had to come inside and if you're not here in ten minutes I am going to just start walking home. And then I'll get hit by a car, and everyone will be really sad, you'll be sad, whoever hit me will be sad, Mary Anne'll be sad and then you'll have to bury my body. In the *ground*.

> *Beat.*

Just please come get me unless you want to scar me forever. I'm in the computer lab. Bye.

> *She tosses the phone in her bag.*
>
> *She turns to look at the sleeping computers, her friends.*

She peers around to make sure no one is looking, then makes her way to her favorite computer by the window. She reaches for a disc in her bag, pops it in, and the game begins.

A smile crosses her face. This game soothes her. It's one of the few things that makes her happy.

GAME & JANE. *(Booming.)* THE OREGON TRAIL!

GAME. You may:

One: Travel the trail.

Two: Learn about the trail.

What is your choice?

JANE. *(Clicking.)* Travel that shit.

GAME. Many kinds of people made the trip to Oregon.

JANE. No der.

GAME. You may:

One: Be a banker from Boston.

Two: Be a carpenter from Ohio.

Three: Be a farmer from Illinois.

Four: Be a completely ineffectual middle-schooler who has yet to excel at anything and who also cannot manage her body odor.

JANE. That one's new.

Carpenter because they can fix the wagon axle things!

Punching a key.

Carpenterrrrrrr!

GAME. What is the first name of the wagon leader?

JANE. *(Typing.)* Me, duh! Jane.

GAME. What are the first names of the four other members in your party?

JANE. Jared!

Blossom!

Claire Danes!

Anddddddd...

> *The cursor blinks.*

Billy.

GAME & JANE. *(Booming.)* GOING BACK TO 1848.

> *Jane's big sister,* **MARY ANNE**, *seventeen, passes by. She's effortlessly pretty, seemingly perfect, and carries a violin in a case. She's a bit manic, constantly covering something she's not old enough to yet name.*

MARY ANNE. What're you doing? You're supposed to be out front. Mom said to meet her out front so you need to be out front.

JANE. She's already like 100 years late which is so stupid because she doesn't even have a *job.*

MARY ANNE. Neither do you.

JANE. Neither do you.

MARY ANNE. *We're* her job.

JANE. I'm not a job! I'm self-sufficient, I trim my own bangs.

MARY ANNE. Yeah, and it shows.

> **MARY ANNE** *goes to* **JANE**, *messes with her bangs, trying to straighten them.*

JANE. Stop it!

MARY ANNE. Just hold still, I'm just – there.

> **JANE***'s bangs are now smoothed across her face like a Catholic orphan child.*
>
> **JANE** *smiles at* **MARY ANNE** *angelically – then messes them up again. Take that.*
>
> **JANE** *turns back to her game. Game music resumes.*
>
> **MARY ANNE** *goes back to fixing her sister's hair.*

Are you playing that by choice?

JANE. I wanna beat it but computer class always ends. But I'm going to.

MARY ANNE. It's such a pointless game.

JANE. YOU'RE a pointless game.

MARY ANNE. No I'm not.

JANE. I am learning valuable life skills.

MARY ANNE. Like what?

JANE. Hunting.

MARY ANNE. Yeah, what're you gonna hunt?

JANE. Someday I could need to.

MARY ANNE. We had ancestors on the trail, I think.

> *She then gets a brilliant idea. Reaches into*
> *her bag for notebook and pencil, jots down*
> *her thoughts as she has them, endless lists,*
> *boxes to check.*

That should be my college essay. 2500 words. How the trail life informed my current life in a time I faced a true test of character. That's so good.

I should minor in history, in college –

> **MARY ANNE**'s *mind zips into the future.*

JANE. Can I have a dollar?

MARY ANNE. What for?

JANE. Vending machine.

MARY ANNE. Jane, soda is SO bad for you. For your teeth, for your skin, for your mid-section, also for your hair I think –

JANE. My body my choice and my choice is a Mountain Dew.

MARY ANNE. You have got to build good habits now. If you're not careful you'll get really fat in college.

JANE. That's like in 100 years.

MARY ANNE. Which is sooner than you think.

> **MARY ANNE** *smells* **JANE**. *Makes a face.*

JANE. ...What?

MARY ANNE. Nothing.

JANE. Do I smell?

MARY ANNE. A little bit.

JANE. *(Horrified.)* What kind?

MARY ANNE. Like you've been running.

JANE. I haven't been running, I don't run, it's just how I smell.

> **MARY ANNE** *starts to rummage through her bag.*

MARY ANNE. You gotta start wearing deodorant. Mom got you some Teen Spirit, you gotta start *using* / it or people are gonna keep saying things –

JANE. I DO, I DO USE IT.

MARY ANNE. I'm not – I'm just trying to help.

JANE. Well you're not.

MARY ANNE. If you wanna make friends / you have to –

JANE. I have friends! They're back at Whitaker!

MARY ANNE. Well, you go *here* now.

JANE. Why did we have to *move*.

> **MARY ANNE** *pulls out some terrible spray, sprays it all over her sister.*

Ahhhh STOP it!

Now I smell like Bath and Body Works freaking died in my hair!

MARY ANNE. You smell *better*. You smell like –

> *She looks at the bottle. She isn't sure.*

– honeysuckles at sunset – melon.

JANE. I smell like a whore baby.

> **MARY ANNE** *sprays herself so she too smells like honeysuckle melons at sunset.*

MARY ANNE. You gotta take care of yourself, you gotta pay attention to yourself.

You should let Mom take you shopping for some new clothes!

JANE. If I ever had a scrunchie that matched my shirt I would kill myself.

MARY ANNE. But maybe if you felt *better* about your *appearance*, then –

JANE. *(Quickly.)* Guys don't like me.

MARY ANNE. Yeah they do.

JANE. Who?

> *Beat.*

MARY ANNE. But also, who cares? It doesn't matter.

JANE. I wanna go home. Why can't you just drive me it'll take like two seconds!

MARY ANNE. I have lessons 'til five.

JANE. *(Groaning.)* Guhhhhhhhhhh I'm going to kill myself.

> *Beat.*

MARY ANNE. You shouldn't joke about that. It's not funny.

JANE. I'm not laughing!

MARY ANNE. It's a very serious subject. Didn't they show you the video in health class?

JANE. Yeah so I'm obviously not serious or I'd be giving away all my CDs.
It's just words. They're all I have.

> *Beat.*

MARY ANNE. What's going on with you? Ever since you got your / period

JANE. Don't say p–

MARY ANNE. You've been all –

JANE. I *know*.

> *Beat.*

> I think when you get your p– when you get it – it's like when your body starts to tell you the truth about your life.

MARY ANNE. No, Jane, it is a reproductive / cycle that –

JANE. DON'T SAY CYCLE.

MARY ANNE. Well that's what it is!

> *Beat.*

JANE. Sometimes – when things are – quiet? And still? Something so – heavy and so – sad – comes out of nowhere. And it just sits on me. Even when everything is okay.

 Beat.

You ever feel it? Even way deep down?

MARY ANNE. *(Uncomfortable.)* No.

JANE. *(Almost to herself.)* What is it?

MARY ANNE. I don't know.

I have to get to practice. If I'm late Mr. Parham makes me do scales.

 MARY ANNE *goes. She stops by the door.*

JANE. What happened to them?

MARY ANNE. What?

JANE. To our people on the trail? Did they make it?

 MARY ANNE *is still lost in her own future plans.*

MARY ANNE. ...I don't know.

 She goes.

JANE. *(After her.)* Don't get hit by a car.

Because then I would be the girl whose sister died.

And then people would feel sorry for me.

And then I would have a name for whatever this is. "Loss."

 She turns back to game.

 The cursor blinks.

Continue on the Trail.

 The music resumes.

GAME. That was your SISTER?
DAMNNNNNN.

JANE. Continue on the TRAIL.

GAME. 1848. INDEPENDENCE, MISSOURI.

Lights warm to include **THEN JANE**, *staring suspiciously at a wagon.*

She is a prairie girl with once-tight braids that are falling out.

The wagon is not a cartoon version of the trailblazer, but like the actual thing, a Conestoga built from light, sturdy wood to carry a medium to light load.

This is not a game or cartoon, this is real.

Her father, **CLANCY**, *and her cheery as shit sister,* **MARY ANNE**, *stand next to the wagon.*

THEN JANE. ...You wanna do *what*?

CLANCY. We're gonna head West, daughter!

MARY ANNE. *(So excited.)* To Oregon City!

THEN JANE. Why'd you tell her and not me?

MARY ANNE. I'm the oldest, Jane, I get the first wave of information, it's logic, strict.

CLANCY. We're gonna join your Uncle Elijah. Got post from 'im, says there's free land in Oregon.

320 acres a free land for every man.

MARY ANNE. My letter from cousin Joseph says RIVERS and FORESTS.

THEN JANE. What're we gonna do with 320 acres of land?!

CLANCY. Gonna farm it!

MARY ANNE. We're gonna grow COTTON or CORN! And we're gonna build a new HOUSE! With a sittin' room – a wash room – a room just for books – a sittin' room for guests – gentlemen guests – a whole cold room for just cheese –

THEN JANE. You're a *carpenter*, Pa. How're you gonna grow a thing?

CLANCY. I can learn! Your Uncle Elijah said he'd teach me. If they can teach the Injuns howta, I can learn it, too.

MARY ANNE. Jane, look at the positive.

THEN JANE. I'm tryin' ta but I just don't see it.

CLANCY. *(Firm.)* Find it, and look at it.

    Beat.

THEN JANE. I guess I once dreamt I were the type that longed for adventure.

CLANCY. There ya go!

THEN JANE. But that wagon's kinda small.

CLANCY. Shore's smaller than others, but we only need two oxen ta pull this fella.

I know she ain't the best but she was all I could get for Lucy.

THEN JANE. What happened to Lucy?!

CLANCY. She ain't dead, daughter, she just don't belong to us anymore. Simple as that. I traded her.

THEN JANE. What?! Why didn't you tell me so I could say goodbye?!

CLANCY. 'Cause you're the sensitive type and I know you woulda drug out the farewell.

Lucy was a cow, daughter, t'weren't a person.

THEN JANE. Well how would we fit all our things insida there?

MARY ANNE. We'll havta sell some of it, Pa says. Only bring with us the precious and important items.

Then when we get west, fresh start!

THEN JANE. I wanna die.

CLANCY. Careful what you wish for there, daughter. Don't tempt God, now.

MARY ANNE. Don't be glum, Jane, we're gonna see ALL the territories! All of the fabrics and all the flowers and all the cultures and all the fields and all the little rabbits, I bet each new state is different, with a different type a land, a different type a tree –

THEN JANE. Or maybe it all looks like Missoura so why leave?

CLANCY. Listen ta me.

Your ma – she woulda wanted us to join her family, and Oregon's where they are.

There's a whole new life for us out there. Nothin' left for us in Independence.

THEN JANE. This is where I've grown up. This is where my roots are.

CLANCY. S'true.

But I gotta – I need a change, daughters.

Everywhere I look I still see your ma.

> **THEN JANE** and **MARY ANNE** *are quiet at this rare and potent glimpse of* **CLANCY**'s *emotion.*

I walk past the post e'ry day I see the hill where she's buried, and my folks buried, my sister and my brother and my brother's wife. Each day I wanna stop and – I wanna rest there, for a moment.

THEN JANE. Well then you should.

CLANCY. Don't got time for that. Each day? For that sort of reflection? No, ma'am. Gotta move on.

Please trust that I know what's best for ya.

I'm tryin' to change your life here, now.

I gifted it to ya and now you gotta trust me with it.

You'll thank me someday, daughter.

> *Beat.*

THEN JANE. ...How long will it take to get there?

CLANCY. Got about two thousand miles to go – Elijah says you can make 'bout fifteen miles a day –

MARY ANNE. Ooh! Ooh!

> *Quick math.*

Carry the – four months! Four!

CLANCY. That's right.

THEN JANE. *Months?* I don't agree with this.

CLANCY. I'm not askin' you your opinion, daughter, I'm tellin' you my plans. It's decided.

Now. We gotta get on. If we move through the night we can catch up with the group left a few days ago. Now go help your sister, start packin' up.

MARY ANNE. OH PA, CAN I BRING MY FIDDLE? CAN I?

CLANCY. 'Course you can.

>> **CLANCY** *goes.*

>> **MARY ANNE** *inspects the sky.*

MARY ANNE. Rain's comin' in. Come on. Help me with the packin'.

I'm going to put everything in boxes and take my pencil and write on each box what's inside of each box. That way when we get to the promised land –

THEN JANE. Has it been promised?

MARY ANNE. ...When we get there, we'll take all of the boxes out of the wagon and there will be a box for each room and the name will be on the box. And we'll take that box into that room and unpack it and it'll all make such pretty sense.

>> *She takes a deep, soothing breath.*

THEN JANE. I'm going to go behind you to all of the boxes and erase all the names.

MARY ANNE. Don't you dare.

>> **MARY ANNE** *starts packing obsessively.*

THEN JANE. Can you imagine a world with no boxes?

I want you to stand right there and imagine that world.

>> **MARY ANNE**, *ignoring her, produces her fiddle.*
>> *She starts to play, calming herself.*

MARY ANNE.
>> LOU LOU
>> SKIP TO MY LOU
>> LOU LOU
>> SKIP TO MY LOU
>> LOU LOU
>> SKIP TO MY LOU
>> SKIP TO MY LOU MY DARLING

THEN JANE. You done?

MARY ANNE.
>> LOU LOU
>> SKIP TO MY LOU

LOU LOU
SKIP TO MY LOU
LOU LOU
SKIP TO MY LOU MY DARLING

Back to the computer lab.

GAME. It is 1848. Your jumping-off place for Oregon is Independence, Missouri.

You must decide which month to leave Independence.

One: March.

Two: April, when the world is full of dresses and popsicles and possibility.

Three: May, when the sun starts to smolder and your bangs stick to your face no matter what you do, and you are disgusting.

JANE. I'm growing them out!

GAME. Four: Ask for advice.

What is your choice?

JANE. April 'cause of less hot months and you skip storm season.

GAME. Before leaving Independence, you should have equipment and supplies.

JANE. Really? 'Cause I was going to traverse the country with NOTHING!

GAME. Just as you are unequipped to traverse life.

JANE. Touché, game.

GAME. You have 800 dollars in cash, but you don't have to spend it all now.

You can buy whatever you need at Matt's General Store. Press space bar to continue.

JANE. Hi Matt. Will you be my boyfriend, Matt?

GAME. That is not the answer!

JANE. Is it part of the answer?

GAME. I cannot tell you!

JANE. What. Is. It.

GAME. Cannot reveal!

Resuming.

MATT'S GENERAL STORE. INDEPENDENCE, MISSOURI.

March 1, 1848.

> *Matt's General Store.* **MARY ANNE** *and* **THEN JANE** *wait as* **CLANCY** *orders supplies.*

MATT. What can I get for ya?

JANE & CLANCY. 800 pounds of food.

JANE. Blow Pops. Cheez-Its. Guns.

CLANCY. Flour, sugar, bacon, coffee.

JANE & CLANCY. One yoke of oxen.

MATT. Good choice. They spook less easy than horses, tire less too.

I got some right strong ones for ya. Don't need oats, just grass.

MARY ANNE. I'm gonna give each oxen a name suited to their personality. Each day I'm gonna note characteristics of each oxen, and select a name from the universe that corresponds with their nature!

MATT. Shore, they'll like that. Just make sure they get their water or they might go crazy 'n' run you off a ravine! Straight to your death!

> *Hearty laughter.*

What else can I get for ya?

JANE. Ten boxes of bullets for those pesky Injuns and wolves.

JANE & CLANCY. Wagon wheel, wagon axel, wagon tongue, two of each.

> **MATT** *hefts and lifts and presents them with each part.*

MATT. Here ya are.

These parts'll start ya. Once you get to Fort Kearny you can trade for more.

And if ya come across a wagon that's been abandoned, it's trail rules you can pillage it for parts, if ya need be, 'cause chances are, those folks're dead! And make sure ya boil your drinking water or you might catch the Cholera!

> *Again, they all laugh, but less. More so just – politely avoiding the reality of their potentially impending doom.*

CLANCY. This'll do us, Matt. We thank you kindly.

MATT. Good luck, Clancy. I wish luck to you all.

MARY ANNE. And we wish luck to *you*!

CLANCY. We'll send letters.

THEN JANE. No we won't.

MATT. Oh yeah, why not?

THEN JANE. Because we'll never make it.

Because America ends after Missoura. It drops off like the lip of a table into a fiery sea. Because there is no place in the world but Missoura, where what's left a my ma's body lay in the ground.

> *Beat.*

MATT. Well, watch out for bears!

> *They all laugh heartily, except for* **THEN JANE**.

You're ready to start. Good luck! You have a long and difficult journey ahead of you!

JANE. Thanks Matt! Clearly you have feelings for me.

GAME. Now loading the wagon...

> **MARY ANNE** *and* **CLANCY** *load the wagon.*
>
> **THEN JANE** *drags on a large and beautiful rocking chair.*
>
> **CLANCY** *spots it – the sight of it saddens him.*

THEN JANE. We almost forgot Ma's chair.

CLANCY. We're all full up, daughter.

THEN JANE. But shouldn't we keep something a hers? For remembrance sake?

> **MARY ANNE** *runs her hands over the wood, remembering.*

MARY ANNE. Oh Pa – is it true that when you made this very nursin' chair for Ma when she was full a me was when you *knew* you wanted to be a carpenter?

THEN JANE. Thank you for the exposition.

MARY ANNE. I just like remembering that. It's a good memory that I'm fond of.

CLANCY. 'Strue. But we don't got room. Get west, I'll make you a hundred rockin' chairs.

THEN JANE. So we're just gonna leave it back here like she never was?!

> *This lands on* **MARY ANNE**, *makes her sad, but she shakes it off.*

MARY ANNE. *(Diverting.)* She's watchin' us from heaven and she's in our hearts. And the framed likeness a her will go on the mantle, first thing.

THEN JANE. *(Desperate.)* Pa. *Please.*

CLANCY. Time to get going.

> **MARY ANNE** *happily gets into the wagon.*

MARY ANNE. Jane, c'mon. It's actually kinda nice in here! It's kinda cozy! It's like a little house inside, it's like a little story!

THEN JANE. STOP. TALKIN'.

CLANCY. 'Bout to be a real crimpy night, we gotta get goin'. Get in.

THEN JANE. Nope. Not gone do it, Pa.

> **CLANCY** *stares at his daughter, who won't budge, who clings to her mother's chair.*

CLANCY. GET IN THE WAGON, JANE.

THEN JANE. I'm staying here, independent.

CLANCY. You are getting in this wagon if I have to throw you in it and tie you to it.

THEN JANE. That's abuse.

CLANCY. Not abuse if I fathered you.

THEN JANE. I hate you.

CLANCY. *(Hard.)* Hate me from inside this wagon! Go on!

>*Pissed,* **THEN JANE** *crawls into the wagon.*

>*From inside:*

MARY ANNE. So that part's my room, and that part's *your* room, and there's the parlor –

THEN JANE. Smells like old potatoes in here.

CLANCY. Good. That's the old potatoes.

THEN JANE. Smells like tears.

>**CLANCY** *starts to mount the front of the wagon – but spots the rocking chair resting there in the dirt. He exhales. A part of him doesn't want to leave it either, this thing he made that once held his daughter and wife.*

>*He picks up the chair, ties it to the top of the wagon. It's sloppy, but it'll do.* **THEN JANE** *sees this.*

(Breathless.) Thank you – thank you, Pa –

GAME. Here you are, you're ready to go! Care to say farewell?

JANE. Fine! Bye, see you never.

>**CLANCY** *readies his oxen.*

>*Before he proceeds, he stops to pray.*

CLANCY. Dear Lord I have often doubted but I know is there:

>*Beat. He looks up the trail that awaits them.*

I know there have been – dark hours.

Hours when I din't know how to carry on.

When Abigail up and got sick. Never woke up.

When all I see is loss and most everyone I loved choking out their last bits of life.

Drownin'. Fevers. Carryin' on.

But I got these daughters, here. You give me these daughters, here.

Gotta go on for them.

And so I ask you to put in all of us the will to go on, no matter how rough.

That is our *nature*, that you have given us. To keep goin'.

And we thank you for that blessing.

Amen.

MARY ANNE. *(Suddenly, from inside wagon.)* AMEN.

> *A hawk flies by, crying like an omen.*
>
> **CLANCY** *faces the town one last time.*

CLANCY. Farewell, Missoura!

MARY ANNE. Farethee well!

THEN JANE & JANE. Goodbye, forever.

> **CLANCY** *goes to his oxen, driving them.*

CLANCY. HAW! HAW!

> *They begin their mile, the first of thousands, as night falls.*

GAME. Independence, Missouri. March 1, 1848.

You may:

One: Continue on the Trail.

Two: Check supplies.

Three: Hitchhike home, which will make a great story to tell in adulthood, over and over and over, after six of your drinks of choice.

Four: Walk to the gas station, and steal and eat your weight in Charleston Chews.

What is your choice?

JANE. The gas station is really far.

Continue on the Trail.

GAME. Continuing on the Trail.

> *The travelers move through the dust, persevere, push forward.*

Billy has a snakebite.

JANE. Aww man –

GAME. Continuing on the trail.

You have lost Billy.

Here lies Billy.

JANE. So sad. Now we'll never marry.

Syke. I'd marry you even if you were DEAD.

> *Suddenly,* **BILLY** *passes by. He is the hottest prepubescent dude this school has to offer, the kind of hot that, in retrospect, was really not that hot at all. It was just that perfect flip of hair, the perfect sag of the soccer shorts.*

> *He comes up behind* **JANE.** *His mid-practice sweat drips onto the keyboard.*

BILLY. *(Looking at screen.)* No way, I died?!

> *Clearly this is the first time* **BILLY** *has addressed* **JANE** *in a year, though she's dreamt of it happening multiple times and it's usually happening inside of an Abercrombie and Fitch against a rack of jean jackets that smell of Woods.*

> **JANE** *pauses the game.*

JANE. No, um – it wasn't you. I didn't name it after you.

BILLY. Yeahhhh, there's lots of Billys.

JANE. No they're not, you're the only one!

> *Beat.*

BILLY. So what's up bus buddy?

JANE. I'm your bus buddy?

BILLY. Well you were before I got my license. Boom.

> *He whips his license out of his pocket, so proud, and shows it to her.*

Official member of the great state of Oregon.

Nailed it on the first try.

JANE. Cool. I saw your car, the wheels're really big.

BILLY. Yeah, I lifted that shit.

Yeah, it's a great car, yeah. I did the down payment myself with my job money. I got a job. My dad was gonna get me one, but then I was like, hell nah, I can get it for myself, I don't want your money.

> **BILLY** *stops, suddenly feeling he's revealed too many feelings.*

So whatever.

JANE. I miss seeing you on the, I mean I miss talking to you on the, I mean I haven't / talked to you in –

BILLY. What?

JANE. Nothing.

BILLY. So what's your deal? When I see you you always look so sad.

JANE. This is just my face.

BILLY. Cool, so what're you still doing here?

JANE. My mom's late picking me up.

BILLY. Sucks, yeah.

I'd give you a ride home when I'm done but I gotta meet my buddy after practice.

JANE. You would?

BILLY. Yeah man, we're neighbors right?

JANE. Yeah. I just got a trampoline.

That we could jump on sometime. Simultaneously.

That means at the same time.

BILLY. Yeah, sounds good, your sister's Mary Anne Goodrich, yeah?

JANE. Yeah.

BILLY. Cool, cool. She seems cool.

Aw man, Coach has been killing us, man, we're running laps. We're on a ten. I think I pulled a hammie.

> *He stretches. Yay.*

> *He drinks his Gatorade, his Adam's apple bobbing.* **JANE** *takes in this glorious sight.*

*He then takes a load off in the wheely chair
next to her, wheels in close to her.*

BILLY. How far're you?

JANE. What?

BILLY. In the game.

JANE. Oh, pretty far, / I –

BILLY. Man. I always get dysentery.

JANE. *(Boldly.)* I'm really good at it.

    Then.

The game. Not at getting dysentery.

It's good to be a carpenter 'cause you start with more money and you have more skills.

And don't pick farmer 'cause then you're really poor.

BILLY. Cool, so what happens at the end?

JANE. Oh um. I've never gotten to the end.

I bet you're just – there. And probably most of your family is dead. But you have character.

BILLY. Cool, cool, so what's your sister's deal?

JANE. *(Not getting it.)* What's her deal how?

BILLY. *(Gee, I'd like her to take my virginity.)* Like what's her deal?

JANE. She sucks, she's okay.

BILLY. Cool, cool. Just wondering, whatever.

    Beat.

What time is it, I gotta head out –

JANE. *(Suddenly bold.)* Your dad's an idiot.

    Beat.

Sorry, um. My mom is friends with your mom. They do Jazzercise together.

So I heard, about.

    Beat.

He's an idiot for leaving.

    Beat.

And that's all I have to say about that.

BILLY. *(Weirdly touched.)* Yeah.

He showed up at one of my games and I was like. Whatever.

I think I'm like, traumatized.

> **JANE** *hears this. This is the hottest thing she has ever heard.* **BILLY** *blossoms in front of her into Jordan Catalano, damaged, hair in his eyes.*

JANE. *(Breathless.)* Yeah.

> *Then.*

Well look at the bright side.

Now you have something to overcome. Instead of just like, being fine. Which is the real tragedy.

BILLY. Who says?

JANE. Me. Just now.

> **BILLY** *smiles, feeling strangely understood.*
>
> **JANE** *cannot believe this is happening, this conversation. She wants to make a home inside of it.*

BILLY. What're you gonna put on my tombstone?

JANE. I – I don't know –

BILLY. Put something awesome on it. Here, I'll do it.

> *He leans over her to type and she dies the middle school death of longing and lust.*

Pepperoni.

> *He laughs.*

JANE. Ha ha – pizza joke!

> *They laugh together.*

BILLY. Wait, hold on –

> *He leans over her farther, typing.*

And – sausage.

> *When he brings his hand back he accidentally touches* **JANE**'s *boobs.*

BILLY. Whoa, sorry.

JANE. *(Bold.)* I'm not.

> *Compelled by something,* **JANE** *leans in and kisses him, which she's never done, and has learned mostly from episodes of* My So-Called Life.
>
> *He pushes her off, reels back, repelled, horrified, like his sister just kissed him.*

BILLY. That was weird.

JANE. I – sorry – I thought –

BILLY. Uh, I gotta head out.

> *He heads for the door.*

JANE. But if you ever wanna come over / and jump on the trampoline –

> *But she just sits there.*
>
> **BILLY** *goes.*
>
> **JANE** *turns back to her computer, his smell lingering on her, her heart racing. She is quietly horrified and devastated.*

GAME. YOU HAVE REACHED THIS MOMENT.
WOW, THAT JUST HAPPENED.
OH MAN.
YOU REALLY PUT YOURSELF OUT THERE. WAY TO GO.
BUT YOU SHOULD PROBABLY NEVER DO THAT AGAIN.
You may:
One: Wallow in this moment
Two: Write a poem about this moment
Three: Move past this moment. What is your choice?

JANE. ...Wallow.

GAME. You have chosen to wallow in this moment.

> **JANE** *reaches into her backpack, finds and puts on her Discman. Selects a track.*
>
> *It's something like Bush's "Glycerine."* *
>
> *She sings, badly, with full heart.*
>
> **THEN JANE**, *trailing behind the wagon, joins her, exhausted, singing the same song to herself.*

MARY ANNE. *(From offstage.)* Jane? What is that nonsense you're singing?

THEN JANE. Dunno.

> *Outside, a car horn Honks and Honks.*
>
> **JANE** *ejects the disk, shoves it in her bag.*

JANE. I'M COMING!!

> **THEN JANE**, **MARY ANNE**, *and* **CLANCY** *are frozen.*
>
> *Gradually they turn to dust and blow away with the wind.*
>
> **JANE** *heads toward the door, but – she is stopped. Trapped. Suddenly:*

GAME. *(Booming.)* GOING FORWARD IN TIME.

JANE. But – I'm not playing right now –

GAME. Many kinds of people live their lives.

You may:

One: Continue to sit in the middle of your Life and Wallow in it.

Two: Sit in the shadow of your sister's life.

Three: Live your life.

---

*A license to produce *The Oregon Trail* does not include a performance license for "Glycerine." The publisher and author suggest that the licensee contact ASCAP or BMI to ascertain the music publisher and contact such music publisher to license or acquire permission for performance of the song. If a license or permission is unattainable for "Glycerine," the licensee may not use the song in *The Oregon Trail* but should create an original composition in a similar style or use a similar song in the public domain. For further information, please see Music Use Note on page 3.

JANE. ...Live it?

GAME. GOING FORWARD IN TIME!

Most people graduate high school.

You may spend high school:

One: Being focused on your studies and excelling academically.

Two: Being focused on attention from boys but never getting it.

Three: Doing drama club and getting cast as boy parts because there are too many girls.

Four: A combination of Two and Three.

JANE. Definitely the focusing on my studies one?

GAME. Number One is not an option.

JANE. You just said it was an option.

GAME. Number One is not an option.

Please select another option and press space bar to continue.

JANE. A combination of Two and Three?

GAME. You have forged high school.

You have lost your virginity.

JANE. How?

GAME. Dysentery.

JANE. Can I start / over?

GAME. *(Booming.)* GOING FORWARD IN TIMEEEEEE.

You have reached college.

JANE. Wait – slow down –

GAME. Most people with the opportunities that your sort of privilege afford attend college.

You may:

One: Attend a well-regarded liberal arts school tucked in the mountains far away where you'll truly find yourself and be the first person since the nineteenth century to make a living as a poet. Driven by the clean mountain air, you start training for marathons, invent pumpkin pie pops and eventually meet and fall in love with a kind and bearded European whom, when you marry him, gifts you with dual citizenship and you live, happily ever after, at home and abroad. You live Everywhere.

Two: Attend a mediocre state school.

What is your choice?

JANE. Definitely One.

GAME. You do not get accepted.

JANE. But –

GAME. Please select an option and press space bar to continue.

JANE. ControlAltDelete. ControlAltDelete.

GAME. You have selected Option Two.

JANE. WAIT –

GAME. GOING FORWARD IN TIMEEEEEE.

You are now in college, would you like to look around?

JANE. ...Fine.

> *We are transported to a college quad.* **JANE** *looks around.*

GAME. What do you want to study? This could determine the rest of your life.

Decide now.

Deciderightnow.

JANE. I don't know / I –

GAME. DECIDE RIGHT NOW.

JANE. Uh – oh, God – I guess I want to take some linguistics, maybe poetry, and French –

GAME. You study Media Studies, which means nothing. Also you gain fifteen pounds.

That fucking food court.

> **JANE** *looks down at her body.*

GOING FORWARD IN TIMEEEEEE.

JANE. Wait – stop –

GAME. You have reached the end of college.

You may:

One: Get a job.

Two: Don't get a job.

JANE. I definitely wanna get / a job –

GAME. CONGRATS YOU GET A JOB.

JANE. Sweet, what job do / I –

GAME. ...I'M SORRY. YOU HAVE BEEN FIRED FROM YOUR JOB.

JANE. ...What?

GAME. DOWNSIZING!

Go home and live with your parents while you "figure things out." Eat their free food and watch their free television.

JANE. I don't wanna play anymore –

GAME. THAT IS NOT AN OPTION. PLEASE SELECT A VALID OPTION.

JANE. Can I try and find another / job –

GAME. USELESS Degree!

You got a USELESS Degree!

Useless Degrees are a PRIVILEGE of the PRIVILEGED!

Please select Option Two.

JANE. I can't get *any* job?

GAME. You are too arrogant for menial labor and also Starbucks!

You sign with a temp agency, instead. You stuff envelopes which barely pays your rent.

So GO HOME AND LIVE WITH YOUR PARENTS.

JANE. Okay, *fine*!

    Beat.

GAME. But your parents do not want you there.

JANE. They don't?

GAME. They do not want to appear to perpetuate your laziness which they otherwise definitely do.

Also, they've just started having sex again!

    Move into your sister's office slash guest room instead!
    Sit in silence, and weep until you can no longer breathe!

JANE. Why am I crying?

GAME. The weight.

    That just comes out of nowhere.

    And sits on you.

        Beat.

JANE. I thought that would go away after middle school.

GAME. IT DID NOT!

JANE. What is it? How do I make / it go away?

GAME. CANNOT REVEAL! WHERE WERE WE? OH RIGHT! Having undergone no real hardships, you have already made a mess of your life and wasted your privilege!

JANE. But – I thought I might make my life mean something.

    No response from the **GAME.**

    Can I go back and try again?

GAME. Never.

    Never.

        Beat.

JANE. I don't wanna be here yet –

GAME. And yet, here you are!

    You have reached your sister's apartment.

JANE. CONTROL – ALT – DELETE.

GAME. Cannot recognize commands.

    Date: Now.

    Weather: Rain. *Cheers* reruns.

    Health: Meh.

    Food: An entire box of Easy Mac and one third bottle of lukewarm chardonnay.

    Next Landmark: Thirty.

    Miles travelled: None except for trips to the pharmacy,

        And he sings!

GAME.

    WHERE EVERYBODY KNOWS YOUR NAME!

    Press space bar to continue.

        Beat.

    Press space bar to continue.

JANE. *(Reluctantly.)* ...Space bar.

PART II

Mary Anne's apartment forms around **JANE**.
*It is well-appointed and optimistic in its
colors, but cluttered with boxes of Jane's
unpacked stuff.*

JANE *has a laptop open on her lap, but she is
staring off into space, listening to her racing
brain. Remnants of her lunch in front of her.
A few dirty dishes.*

*She turns the TV on, to something, anything
to drown out the silence.*

*We hear a recording of a reality fashion
show.*[*]

MARY ANNE, *weary from a long day of working
and doing, enters the apartment. She wears
scrubs.*

She stops for a moment when she sees **JANE** *on
the couch.*

JANE *is surprised to see her. Covers.*

MARY ANNE *sorts through the mail.*

JANE. How's it going, sister?

MARY ANNE. Good! I'm good!

JANE. You're home / early.

MARY ANNE. What're you doing?

JANE. Learning how to roast the perfect sweet potato!
There are a lot of ways.

MARY ANNE. I mean what're you doing home?

JANE. ...Took a personal day.

> **MARY ANNE** *continues to sort through mail.*

---

*A license to produce *The Oregon Trail* does not include a performance
license for any third-party or copyrighted recordings. Licensees should
create their own.

JANE. Hey, did you always know what you wanted to do with your life?

MARY ANNE. Not really, I just did something with it.

> *This stings* **JANE**.

Sorry.

I watched this old woman die today.

JANE. Damn.

MARY ANNE. *(At fridge.)* Did you eat my Lean Cuisine?

JANE. No?

> **MARY ANNE** *shuts the freezer door.*
>
> *Her eyes land on the sink, suspended in space, littered with dishes. She's frustrated but covers, smiles.*

I'm gonna do those later. I had a day.

> **MARY ANNE** *tries to keep her frustration in. Surveys her living room, all of the boxes.*

What're you up to tonight?

MARY ANNE. Nothing.

JANE. You never do nothing.

MARY ANNE. So? I don't know how.

JANE. So nothing means you're going to yoga and also run some errands and do your laundry and start your taxes.

MARY ANNE. *(Sheepish, quiet.)* Yeah and also maybe make some cookies for my boss's birthday.

JANE. Cooookies!! Want / some help?

MARY ANNE. Hey do you think maybe tonight you could unpack your stuff and move it into your room and stuff?

JANE. Yeah. Sorry. I will.

When I have so much time it becomes too much time and I don't know what to do with it because everything I could do with it feels not enough so I end up doing nothing, at all.

You know?

MARY ANNE. Nope, don't know what free time is like, so.

　　MARY ANNE *starts to absentmindedly clean.*

They sure let you take a lot of personal days.

JANE. They're flexible.

MARY ANNE. How flexible?

　　Beat.

JANE. I got let go.

MARY ANNE. You got fired?!

JANE. Let / go.

MARY ANNE. You're a temp, you barely even have to be a person!

JANE. They didn't need me anymore.

And thanks for making me feel like shit on top of already feeling like shit about it.

Speaking of, cat shit on the floor.

　　MARY ANNE *regards the mess.*

MARY ANNE. When?

JANE. What time is it?

　　Silently, **MARY ANNE** *cleans up the mess.*

Sorry, I was gonna clean it up but I didn't know how.

MARY ANNE. "How"?

JANE. I didn't want to mess up your floor.

　　MARY ANNE *cleans.*

Why do you even have a cat, you hate cats!

MARY ANNE. It was Doug's.

When did they fire / you?

JANE. Let me *go.*

MARY ANNE. When?

JANE. Tuesday.

MARY ANNE. Yesterday?

　　Beat.

JANE. Three Tuesdays ago.

MARY ANNE. A MONTH / AGO?

JANE. Three weeks does not a month make.

MARY ANNE. So what, you've just been sitting here?!

JANE. I've been doing stuff!

They let a bunch of people go, it wasn't like some –

MARY ANNE. Why didn't you just tell me?

JANE. Because of your face right now!

MARY ANNE. You want me to smile at you right now?! Here. Yay. Good for you.

> *She forces a smile, placating.*

JANE. I just – I need to take some time to figure out what I really want to do and then like really actively pursue that.

MARY ANNE. Or maybe you need to stop obsessing over whether or not it's the right job, and you just need to *work* so you can pay your rent.

JANE. Mom and Dad said they'd cover next month.

MARY ANNE. But maybe you should stop expecting them to pay for things?

JANE. They owe me.

MARY ANNE. How?

JANE. Trauma.

MARY ANNE. Okay, that's – I'm not going to respond to that.

> **MARY ANNE** *starts to stack magazines aggressively.*

JANE. *(Trying.)* I've been looking online! For jobs. I responded to 900 posts. I don't even know if my e-mails are even getting opened though.

MARY ANNE. That's why you have to follow up.

JANE. Yeah but my résumé sucks. It's like, "Went to high school. Went to college. Made a few sandwiches. Cried a few times."

MARY ANNE. Well then think about your strengths, and beef it up.

JANE. Yeah.

>*Beat.* **MARY ANNE** *is glaring at her.*

You mean like right now?

MARY ANNE. Yeah.

JANE. Okay. Here I go.

>**JANE** *doesn't move, eyes glued to her computer.*
>
>**MARY ANNE** *looks over her shoulder.*

I'm doing it!

MARY ANNE. You're on / Facebook.

JANE. I'M NETWORKING!

>**MARY ANNE** *gives her a look.*

I'm gonna unpack first.

MARY ANNE. Are you?

JANE. Yes. I am.

>**MARY ANNE** *goes to bed.*
>
>**JANE**, *alone.*
>
>*She goes to a box.*
>
>*Sinks to the ground. Opens it.*
>
>*Starts to dig through it.*
>
>*CDs, notes, scrapbooks, trophies. It's all too depressing.*
>
>*She opens another. She finds her Discman. Sweet.*
>
>*She keeps digging. It's all too depressing.*
>
>*She returns to the couch, to her computer. Lies on her back, scrolls and scrolls.*
>
>*Suddenly, her eyes light up.*

GAME. You can now play the Oregon Trail online for free! Get yer wagon ready and let's hit the trail!

JANE. Yes pleaseeeeee.

>*Eagerly, she clicks.*

The green from the game screen lights her face
as it explodes into a nostalgic smile. Game
music resumes.

GAME. HELLO AGAIN.

JANE. Hello to you too.

GAME. You look exactly the same but older.

JANE. You look weird now. I liked you better before.

GAME. Oh look, your boobs are the exact same size. Is that weird for you?

JANE. Could we just –

GAME. The Oregon Traillllllllll!

You may:

One: Read the news. Become a more grounded and intelligent person.

Two: Sign up to give a micro loan to struggling single mothers in developing nations, you great person you!

JANE. I wanna finish this game.

GAME. You are technically an adult technically! Do you really want to finish this game right now?

JANE. *(Determined, firm.)* I am going to finish this game.

GAME. Fine. You have selected to stay inside and regress to your childhood and be one of those people who finds corn chips in their hair and then eats them. Okay, great. You may:

One: Start a new game.

Two: Resume your old game.

JANE. Start a new game.

GAME. That is not an option.

JANE. You just / said –

GAME. That. Is not. An option.

JANE. Fine. Resume.

GAME. CONTINUING ON THE TRAILLLLLLLL!

We find the family trudging up the trail, some
weeks later. They are weary, worn-down,

exhausted. Dust whips into their eyes, the sun burns and blisters their lips.

The wagon moves through shrubs and dust. Eventually **THEN JANE** *and* **MARY ANNE** *get out and follow behind it. The wheels whine. They are going and going but it seems like they've gotten nowhere.*

Their feet and the wheels sink into dust.

MARY ANNE.
TURKEY IN THE STRAW
TURKEY IN THE HAY
TURKEY IN THE STRAW
TURKEY IN THE HAY
ROLL 'EM UP AND TWIST 'EM UP
A HIGH TUCK A-HAW
AND HIT 'EM UP A TUNE CALLED TURKEY IN THE STRAW

Beat.

TURKEY IN THE STRAW
TURKEY IN THE HAY
TURKEY IN THE STRAW
TURKEY IN THE HAY
ROLL 'EM UP AND TWIST 'EM UP
A HIGH TUCK A-HAW
AND HIT 'EM UP A TUNE CALLED TURKEY IN THE STRAW

THEN JANE. I sure wish there *was* a turkey in the straw. I'm so sick a beans.

MARY ANNE. Did that sound good Pa? I'm getting better! Figure I'd keep my practicing up –

CLANCY. Sounded real nice.

C'mon, let's get a move on, pick it up. Just 'til dusk then we'll make camp. Feelin' wolfish.

THEN JANE. Where's the other party, Pa?

CLANCY. We'll find 'em.

THEN JANE. We lost track a their trail days ago.

CLANCY. ...We'll find 'em, Jane.

THEN JANE. What if we don't?

MARY ANNE. You gotta keep your spirits up!

> *They walk.* **CLANCY** *directs the oxen around a bend.*

CLANCY. Gee! *(Right.)*

Haw! *(Left.)* I said HAW! HAW!

> *They keep moving, dragging their feet through the dust.*

MARY ANNE. I like to slice time into tiny moments, like little buttons or beads. And then I just take them one by one and I just –

> **THEN JANE** *is just staring at her.*

So that's how I like to think about time.

> *They carry on.*

GAME. You have reached the Platte River.

You must cross the river in order to continue. The river is currently 646 feet across and two-point-three feet deep in the middle.

You may:

One: Attempt to ford the river.

Two: Caulk wagon and float it across.

Three: Get more information.

JANE. *(From couch.)* Ford! Ford! Ford!

> **CLANCY** *inspects the river.*

CLANCY. We'll have ta ford it. No bridge in sight.

> *They attempt to ford. He sweats, pushing on his oxen.*

GET ON NOW! GET ON, BOYS!

MARY ANNE. C'mon Landon! C'mon Bernard!

JANE. *(Playing.)* This is so *hard*.

> *The oxen pull and pull, but the wagon meets quicksand in the middle of the river. It starts to sink.*

> *It's frighteningly real.*

GAME. River is too deep to ford.

CLANCY. No – please God no –

> *Bags of flour, bundles of clothes, boxes of bullets litter the river.*
>
> **MARY ANNE** *nearly drowns as* **CLANCY** *fights through the water, pulling her to safety.*

JANE.

GET THE WARES.

HELP ME.

> **THEN JANE** *struggles through the water, retrieving wares.*
>
> *She drags a bag of flour to shore, collapses on it.*
>
> **CLANCY** *pulls* **MARY ANNE** *to shore, then goes back to the wagon.*
>
> *He unloads wares to lighten the load, then rescues the sinking rocking chair.*
>
> *Finally, the oxen pull the wagon out of the muck.*

GAME. You lose: nine sets of clothing, 890 bullets, two wagon wheels, two wagon axles, one wagon tongue.

CLANCY. Lost a frightful. Help me pack it back up.

THEN JANE. Can't we rest here a moment? Mary Anne near drownded –

MARY ANNE. I'm okay, I'm dandy!

> **MARY ANNE** *coughs up water.* **THEN JANE** *helps her to her feet.*

GAME. What would you like to do?

You may:

One: Continue on the trail.

Two: Stop and rest.

Three: Watch *Extreme Makeover: Home Edition,* the one where half the family's in wheelchairs so they build lots of ramps and you cry.

What is your choice?

JANE. Stop and rest. It's been a long day. You earned it.

> **JANE** *shuts her computer. Turns her attention to the TV.*
>
> *Night falls.*
>
> *Open air, stars.*
>
> **THEN JANE** *sits by a dying fire.*
>
> **CLANCY** *and* **MARY ANNE** *sleep nearby.*
>
> *Faraway wolves, storms.*
>
> **MARY ANNE** *wakes up. She looks radiant. Stretches, adorably.*

MARY ANNE. What're you doin'?

THEN JANE. Can't sleep. Thinkin' all grandly. Too much space out here for thoughts.

MARY ANNE. Pa's gonna hear you and come out here and read you a page from the good book if you don't get to bed.

THEN JANE. 'Mnot hurtin' anybody.

> **MARY ANNE** *joins her.* **THEN JANE** *bursts into tears.*

MARY ANNE. Jane. Stop that!

THEN JANE. I can't.

> **THEN JANE** *tries to dry her eyes on her skirt.*

I miss the house. I miss Lucy.

MARY ANNE. You shouldn't waste time thinkin' about those things.

THEN JANE. Do you miss Ma?

> *Beat. This stings* **MARY ANNE**. *She covers.*

MARY ANNE. She was a long time ago.

THEN JANE. Yeah, but you remember her more than me.

Was Ma – what was her nature?

MARY ANNE. How do you mean?

THEN JANE. Did she laugh often? Was she joyous?

MARY ANNE. She did sometimes.

THEN JANE. But did she –

 Beat.

Did she have – a sorrow in her? Like I do?

MARY ANNE. I don't know what you mean.

THEN JANE. The littlest thing makes me wanna cry. Yesterday I saw a beetle get run over and I felt so sad for its family and I put my tears on into my bonnet. Careful you or Pa didn't see.

MARY ANNE. Good thing, too!

THEN JANE. Sometimes the world makes me so sorrowful, I just –

I just don't know how I'm going to keep going.

I just don't see why.

MARY ANNE. What do you mean *why*?

To move on. To keep goin'.

THEN JANE. But why?

MARY ANNE. ...Because.

THEN JANE. Yeah but why?

MARY ANNE. Because we're alive?

THEN JANE. But why for?

 Beat.

THEN JANE & JANE. Why?

 Beat.

THEN JANE. Why don't we ever talk about her?

MARY ANNE. Well how would that help, if I carried on about it? Waste a strength.

 Beat.

I just think there are other things. To be done. With our time. On this earth. So. That's what I think about that. So.

Hey, we should scrub up tomorrow, you stink.

> *A rustling nearby.*

See? Now you gone and woke Pa.

> **CLANCY** *sits up, tired, pissed, disoriented.*

CLANCY. What'sa matter?

MARY ANNE. Jane says she's "got a sorrow."

CLANCY. Well, you don't. Time to sleep.

THEN JANE. But I'm feeling troubled, genuine.

CLANCY. *(Trying.)* Want me to tell ya a story?

THEN JANE. No thank you.

CLANCY. Aren't you wore out from walkin' all day?

THEN JANE. Sure I'm tired but my heart's not. I'm sad, Pa –

CLANCY. You can't use it as no excuse.

You see to the grease 'n' beans in the morning. You help your sister.

We make beaver early, 'fore sunset.

> *Obediently,* **MARY ANNE** *goes back to her bed.*

> **THEN JANE**'s *tears don't stop.*

I'm not gonna tell you again.

> **CLANCY** *sees his daughter crying. For a moment, he can't help but melt a bit.*

I'm – fond of you, Jane.

THEN JANE. I'm fond of you too.

CLANCY. Yeah. Good.

> *Beat.*

(Breaking slightly.) You got every piece a her. Your ma. You got her nose, you got her fingers, you got the same face when you cry.

THEN JANE. I do?

CLANCY. Spittin' image.

THEN JANE. Do you think about her?

> *Beat. He gathers himself.*

CLANCY. *(Firm.)* Enough a this.

I can't have all this carryin' on.

THEN JANE. Why not?

CLANCY. I – I can't think about it.

THEN JANE. But why / not?

CLANCY. 'S TOO MUCH.

>*Beat.*

Now. We gotta focus on the task at hand, we gotta get ourselves on to Oregon.

THEN JANE. But I don't / want to Pa –

CLANCY. ENOUGH. LISTEN TO ME. You gotta buck up and pull your weight afore I leave you on back with the coyotes. Because I will do that, daughter. Do not test me.

>**THEN JANE** *nods, tears coming. She feels slapped. Stung.*

THEN JANE. *(Weak.)* Okay, Pa –

>**CLANCY** *goes back to sleep.*

>**THEN JANE** *sits alone, studying the stars, her father's words hanging on her.*

>*Lights shift back to Mary Anne's apartment.*

>*The middle of another night. Darker.*

>**JANE** *has changed positions. This time she is lying down, covered in a blanket.*

>*She watches a nature documentary on the Arctic.*

>*A British man drones on about the hardships and survival techniques of various animals.*[*]

>*On the coffee table in front of her her laptop rests, game paused.*

---

*A license to produce *The Oregon Trail* does not include a performance license for any third-party or copyrighted recordings. Licensees should create their own.

JANE. *(Of TV.)* Miraculous...

> MARY ANNE *enters, half-asleep, in sweet pajamas. She's got her glasses on, she's tired and pissed.*

Sorry. Did I wake you up?

MARY ANNE. Yes. Could you turn it down?

JANE. Sorry.

> *She turns it down.*

It's so sad.

MARY ANNE. What.

JANE. The Arctic.

> MARY ANNE *pushes at her temples. Oh my God.*

The winters are so harsh, and – and life has to fight to live. GRASS has to fight. And the caribou – the baby caribou – they can run from predators the moment they're born. It's just in them, when they're born, what is that? And the fox moms have to steal goose babies to feed her OWN babies – it's babies feeding babies – it's so – it's a circle. There's so much pain. But it's necessary.

> MARY ANNE *just stares at her through her bleary eyes. So annoyed.*

MARY ANNE. Hey so, I'm sleeping and you've officially interrupted my REM sleep and I have a twenty-four-hour shift in three hours.

JANE. Sorry. I can't sleep.

MARY ANNE. What time is it?

JANE. *(Looking.)* Almost two.

MARY ANNE. Hey, if you can't sleep, maybe unpack some of your boxes like you said you would do.

JANE. I'm going to start tomorrow.

MARY ANNE. *(To herself.)* Which you said last week.

> JANE *does so.* MARY ANNE *moves sleepily off to the bathroom. She pauses when she sees the dishes, the pile of which has definitely grown.*

JANE. I'm gonna do the dishes before I go to bed.

> **MARY ANNE** *goes into the bathroom. Shuts the door.*

> **JANE***'s eyes return to the TV.*

This polar bear hasn't eaten in four months.
I'll never say I'm hungry ever again.

> *Beat.*

I am so *small.*

> *She turns the TV off.*

> *Then, to no one:*

Why do I feel so –
That's the worst part. It has no name.
It hurts. Right here.

> *She places a hand on her gut.*

And here.

> *She puts a hand on her heart.*

I was gonna do my laundry today but I looked outside
and I saw a lion in the street.

> *Flush.* **MARY ANNE** *re-emerges from the bathroom and heads straight for her room. Door shuts, hard.*

> **JANE** *resumes the* **GAME***, the only thing she feels like doing right now.*

GAME. You have reached this moment.
Another day and you didn't die. Hey: congrats.
You coulda been hit by a car – oh wait.
You did not leave the house today.
Just kidding!
Way to play it safe.
You can:
One: Fester here, in this moment.
Two: Start a blog.
Three: Please. Do not start a blog.

Four: Say it with me.

JANE & GAME. Continue. On. The. Trail.

> **JANE** *sinks farther into the couch as night turns to a beautiful, optimistic morning on the trail.*
>
> *Whimsical clouds.*
>
> **THEN JANE** *sits up, stretches.*
>
> *She observes the sky. A genuine and determined smile spreads across her face.*
>
> *She gets a fire going.*
>
> *She cuts wood. Lugs logs from a stack, focusing intently on her work.*
>
> *She sings a song she should not know, a wondering, pensive song in the style of Blind Melon's "No Rain."* *
>
> **JANE** *sings from the couch, remembering the song, singing listlessly. The song drifts off as* **THEN JANE** *loses focus.*
>
> **THEN JANE** *can't get the fire to light.*

THEN JANE. Shoot. Well, shoot.

GAME. You have a broken spirit. Would you like to try and fix it?

JANE. Sure.

GAME. How would you like to fix it?

One: Unpack a few more boxes therefore earning your sister's love and respect.

---

*A license to produce *The Oregon Trail* does not include a performance license for "No Rain." The publisher and author suggest that the licensee contact ASCAP or BMI to ascertain the music publisher and contact such music publisher to license or acquire permission for performance of the song. If a license or permission is unattainable for "No Rain," the licensee may not use the song in *The Oregon Trail* but should create an original composition in a similar style or use a similar song in the public domain. For further information, please see Music Use Note on page 3.

Two: Respond to this message from Billy Butler from middle school WHICH I STRONGLY DO NOT ADVISE UNLESS OF COURSE YOU LOVE PAIN.

JANE. Wait, say what?

And her phone dings.

She looks. Her face morphs to joy.

BILLY. 'Sup, weary traveller. How long's it been?

You still in town?

We should get a drink sometime.

Here's my number, text it, call it, fax it.

Finally, **THEN JANE** *gets her fire lit. Success.*

JANE *stands, triumphantly.*

PART III

Back on the trail. **THEN JANE** *sets to work making breakfast. Quite the feast.*

Feast cakes, potatoes, venison.

She takes a quenching sip of water from her oil sack.

MARY ANNE *wakes up.*

THEN JANE. Hey sleepyhead! Beautiful morning!

MARY ANNE. ...What're you doin'?

THEN JANE. Makin' breakfast!

MARY ANNE. But I always start breakfast. It's my function.

THEN JANE. Then what's *my* function?

MARY ANNY. I don't know, but you can't have mine!

THEN JANE. I was up early, I thought I'd make it.

MARY ANNE *goes to the fire, inspects.*

MARY ANNE. We're s'posed to be savin' the rest a the venison for the winter!! It's my favorite thing in the winter! Warm venison! It makes me SO. HAPPY.

THEN JANE. We can trade for more, this is a special occasion!

MARY ANNE. Pa's gonna have a storm 'bout this.

PA! PA! JANE'S COOKIN' UP ALL THE MEAT!

CLANCY *emerges from his bed.*

CLANCY. What's all this?

MARY ANNE. JANE's cookin' up all the MEAT!

THEN JANE. It's a special occasion, I told ya!

I have an announcement!

Sit, please. Make me an audience.

CLANCY *and* **MARY ANNE** *reluctantly sit.* **THEN JANE** *serves them coffee.*

This morning I was woke up by the sun.

A pure an' innocent sun. It woke me up like a friend come ask me to play.

I heard what you said to me last night, Pa. You're right. We gotta keep going no matter what.

> **CLANCY** *nods, agreeing, firm, proud.*

And so I announce to you today a new leaf that has turned over.

I – am – attempting happiness.

Please hold your applausing.

> *She smiles.*

MARY ANNE. That's nice but you're burning the last of our meat.

THEN JANE. Shoot.

> **THEN JANE** *attends to the venison.*

> **CLANCY** *kisses the top of her head.*

CLANCY. That's my girl.

MARY ANNE. And me also!

CLANCY. And also you.

> **CLANCY** *and* **MARY ANNE** *settle in for a feast as* **JANE** *finishes up the cooking.*

> *They all eat together, happy, having found this moment of peace among hardship.*

> *Time moves as they eat. We find them full and happy.*

> **MARY ANNE** *grabs her fiddle. Fiddles with it.*

MARY ANNE.
CAMPTOWN LADIES SING THIS SONG
DOO DA! DOO DA!
CAMPTOWN RACETRACK'S TWO MILES LONG!

THEN JANE.
ALL THE DOO DA DAY!

THEN JANE & MARY ANNE.
GOIN' TO RUN ALL NIGHT!
GOIN' TO RUN ALL DAY!
BET MY MONEY ON A BOB-TAILED NAG
SOMEBODY BET ON THE GRAY!

CAMPTOWN LADIES SING THIS SONG
DOO DA! DOO DA!
CAMPTOWN RACETRACK'S TWO MILES LONG!
ALL THE DOO DA DAY!

THEN JANE & MARY ANNE & CLANCY.

GOIN' TO RUN ALL NIGHT!
GOIN' TO RUN ALL DAY!
BET MY MONEY ON A BOB-TAILED NAG
SOMEBODY BET ON THE GRAY!

CAMPTOWN LADIES SING THIS SONG,
DOO DA! DOO DA!
CAMPTOWN RACETRACK'S TWO MILES LONG!
ALL THE DOO DA DAY!
GOIN' TO RUN ALL NIGHT!
GOIN' TO RUN ALL DAY!
BET MY MONEY ON A BOB-TAILED NAG
SOMEBODY BET ON THE GRAY!

They laugh, joyous.

THEN JANE. BERRIES! We need berries for an arbitrary breakfast dessert.
I'll be swift.

She grabs a bucket, goes. **CLANCY** *calls after her.*

CLANCY. Not too far, now!

THEN JANE *goes.* **MARY ANNE** *takes a sip of water from a jug.*

She's a strange girl.

MARY ANNE. I just don't know what's gotten into her.
You want some water, Pa?

CLANCY. Please and thank you.

MARY ANNE *hands him the jug.*

Then:

The back bar of your local Applebee's where the margaritas are face-sized and the potato skins have only been frozen twice.

BILLY, twenty-seven, having grown a gut and a deep awareness of the reality of all things life, sits at the bar, nursing a beer and two whiskies. He stares off. He burps. He stares.

JANE approaches. She's put on a dress and done up her hair.

She spots him immediately.

She can't help it. She smiles, huge. This is the moment. It's finally here.

GAME. You have reached this moment.

You should have worn the better bra, but okay. Sure.

You can:

One: TURN AND RUN AS FAST AS YOU HUMANLY CAN.

Two: Take a step forward. Maybe he's the love of your life.

BILLY burps.

Three: But also maybe not.

Determined, trying to quiet the game, she takes a step forward.

BILLY senses her eyes and turns to her. She tries to play it cool.

BILLY. 'Sup Jane Goodrich.

JANE. Not much, it's great / to –

BILLY. It's two for one apps, we're gettin' double nachos.

JANE. Okay, I'm in!

BILLY. You look great.

JANE. I do?

BILLY. Yeah!

JANE. Yes I do. I look great.

BILLY. Well c'mere! Hug it out, man –

JANE. Yeah, let's do that –

They hug it out, **JANE** *sliding nicely into his nook as she's done so many times in her dreams.*

BILLY. You wanna sit / down?

JANE. Yep! I love to sit. So much better than standing.

She joins him, scooting out a stool.

He slides his whiskey to her.

BILLY. Got this for you.

JANE. Ahhhh thanks. I'm not a big whiskey drinker / but –

BILLY. F that, bottoms up, it's good for your bones.

She takes a sip.

Hey you still play the violin?

JANE. Uh – nope!

That was / my sister –

BILLY. I've been teaching myself the guitar again.

JANE. Nice –

BILLY. Played it a little bit in high school, me and Jared Linville, remember Linville?

JANE. Yeah, totally, with the –

BILLY. Yeah we're starting a band.

JANE. Cool.

She waits for him to ask her what she's been up to, but he does not.

She sips her whiskey. She winces, unaccustomed to it.

Yeah so, I've just been uh – yeah, hanging out. Finished college, went / to –

BILLY. Yeah I did a year at State but messed up my knee, lost my scholarship, started doing some general stuff at Forsyth Tech, gotta get back up with that.

Been working too much though.

JANE. Yeah, where do you work?

BILLY. Home Depot.

JANE. *(Trying.)* Great store.

BILLY. Yeah I help people put their windows and lawn mowers in their cars. It never all fits and they act like it's my fault, but it's not.

They always buy too much shit to fit in their cars.

But my wife doesn't wanna work, so.

JANE. Oh –

BILLY. Remember Ashley, Ashley Shue?

JANE. Yeah, yeah, you two were –? Married?

BILLY. Were.

> *He downs his whiskey, motions for another.*

Separated right now.

JANE. I'm so sorry...

BILLY. Yeah it was going great for a while but now she's a cunt.

GAME. PLEASE LOCATE THE NEAREST EXIT. HAILSTORM AHEAD.

BILLY. Yeah, I don't use that word lightly but it's like, I didn't marry this cunt. She changed.

Happened all the sudden. There was some shit going on with her and some guy.

JANE. Oh man, I'm so sorry –

BILLY. It was good for a while, then, ah –

She just uh, stopped seeing me. Like she used to.

It hurts, you know?

> *He rings his head in his hands, pressing on his temples.*

JANE. I know.

BILLY. I think I'm like. Traumatized.

JANE. Yeah.

BILLY. Yeah, I've been a little depressed actually.

So. That's what's been going on with me.

JANE. That sucks. I'm really sorry to hear that.

BILLY. Yeah.

They drink.

JANE. Like actually depressed?

BILLY. What?

JANE. Like clinically?

BILLY. No, I mean, like.

JANE. Or just – sad.

BILLY. It's not "just"...

JANE. No, yeah, I know. But there's a difference, I think.
I mean – I feel this – my whole life, I've felt this –

She puts a hand to her gut.

Right here. It goes deep. It's not always there.
Sometimes I'm distracted. By work or food or other
people – but when it gets quiet, it's there. And it –
moves? Sometimes it's up in my throat? Even when I
should be happy and good it deepens, it has roots. And
it just – it makes me wanna sob. But I don't think I'm /
depressed per se I just –

BILLY. Least you're not going through a divorce. It's the
fucking worst.

BILLY *drinks.*

I got a son.

JANE. Yeah? I saw some pictures, I wasn't looking or
anything, but I saw –

BILLY. You wanna see?

BILLY *gets out his phone, shows pictures.*

JANE. Aw, he looks just like you –

BILLY. He's my life. Only reason I don't drive my car into
oncoming traffic some days, you know? Scary how easy
that'd be.

JANE. Yeah, to just drive with your eyes closed.

BILLY. Yeah.

Beat.

But I wouldn't / actually.

JANE. Me neither.

BILLY. I want to do something awesome, so he can look at me and be like: I also want to do something awesome. I just wanna be awesome for him.

JANE. Yeah. Pass something down.

BILLY. Exactly.

JANE. All my parents ever gave me was a name.

> *Beat.*

And a trampoline.

And a car.

And college.

BILLY. And *life*, man.

JANE. And life. Yeah. But I feel like I'm wasting whatever life was given to me.

So.

BILLY. Yeah, for sure, for sure.

> *Beat.*

> *Taking her in, with a smile:*

Jane.

JANE. That's me!

BILLY. It's good to see you.

JANE. To the bus!

BILLY. To the bus!

> *They cheers. Drink.* **BILLY** *smiles at* **JANE**, *which emboldens her.*

JANE. Remember seventh grade?

BILLY. Ha, I try not to.

JANE. No, me, seventh grade, you, tenth grade?
The computer lab.

BILLY. Yeah?

JANE. Remember?

BILLY. *(But not.)* I uh – sure?

> *Beat.*

JANE. So you don't?

BILLY. I mean, what're you asking me to remember?

> *Beat.*

JANE. I had this dream about you.

BILLY. Yeah? All right, cool, weird!

JANE. Yeah, um.

I wasn't going to tell you this, but now I'm telling you! Okay. Um.

I was trapped in a building that was burning or falling. Or falling while burning. And you found me.

BILLY. Yeah, cool. And then what?

JANE. You kissed me. And I fell asleep while kissing you.

BILLY. Whoa.

JANE. Yeah. And that thing I feel, was – lifted. It was gone.

> *Beat.*

So I've kind of – it made me wonder if you're – why I feel this.

And if I could – if I could have you –

BILLY. Have me?

JANE. I know it doesn't make sense, but.

> *Beat.*

BILLY. Maybe it does.

JANE. No, I / don't –

BILLY. Only one way to find out.

> *He downs his drink.*

You ready?

JANE. For what?

BILLY. Don't fall asleep.

> *He leans in and he kisses her. It's a nice kiss,*
> *but a kiss that demands a certain result.*

How 'bout that?

JANE. *(Breathless.)* Yeah –

BILLY. You wanna get outta here?

JANE. ...Are you serious?

BILLY. I'm really serious Goodrich, are you serious?

> *She downs her whiskey. She thinks.*

GAME. THIS IS NOT THE ANSWER.

JANE. *(As if there's no choice; as if she's trapped.)* Yeah. Let's go.

> *They go.*
>
> *Back on the trail.*

CLANCY. She should be back by now. She's been gone a long while.

MARY ANNE. *(Off into the distance.)* JANE!

> *Nothing. Faraway storms, wolves.*

CLANCY. JANE!

> *Suddenly, a cloud comes over both of them.*

MARY ANNE. I don't feel so good, Pa –

CLANCY. I just – need to sit –

> *He does. He turns and throws up violently. He stands, trying to regain his strength, but he falls over, back into a pool of his own vomit.*

MARY ANNE. Pa –

> *She goes to him, trying to help him up, but collapses onto him.*
>
> **MARY ANNE** *doubles over in pain, turns, and vomits.*
>
> *A hawk cries as it passes.*
>
> *Then:*
>
> *Mary Anne's apartment.*
>
> *There's an open bottle of nice whiskey on the coffee table. It's been torn into.*
>
> **JANE** *is half-naked, wrapped in a blanket on the couch.*

She looks stunned. Horrified. Processing.

Nearby, **BILLY** *slides on his underwear.*

He chuckles to himself.

BILLY. Girls're turned on by misery, why is that? "Just got separated from my wife," you think they'd head for the hills, man, but no, they're all, *cry on me, fuck me, cry on me –*

>   **JANE** *is speechless.*

People have it too easy now. That's what it is.

Aw man. Jane. You are one dirty birdy.

Full circle, Dirty Birdy. I was comin' for ya.

>   *He laughs and laughs.*

JANE. Why're you – it's not funny –

BILLY. I'm sorry –

JANE. Did you – in my –?

BILLY. What? Yeah, uh –

JANE. I'm not on the –

BILLY. You can take the thing, right, the morning-after thing?

>   **JANE** *does not respond.*

Do you want money for it?

JANE. (*Fighting tears.*) You should go.

BILLY. Yeppp. Was waitin' for that. Okay.

>   *Drunk, he reaches for his terrible jeans, his shoes.*

Was it like your dream?

JANE. No.

BILLY. Well I'm sorry. I can't be that for you, man, I can't fix anyone for shit right now, shit.

>   *He heads for the door.*

Hey don't think I'm like –

I thought this was what we were doing.

JANE. I didn't.

BILLY. Just don't think bad a me, you know? I'm just going through a lot right now, I'm a mess –

'sgood to see you.

> **BILLY** *goes.*

GAME. THAT WAS NOT THE ANSWER.

JANE. What is it. TELL ME WHAT IT IS.

GAME. I CANNOT TELL YOU.

> **JANE** *goes to the computer.*

JANE. WHAT. IS. IT.

GAME. CANNOT REVEAL.

> *She sinks to her knees, destroyed.*
>
> *The sun comes up.*
>
> **JANE** *is on the couch, in the same position, numb.*
>
> **MARY ANNE** *enters – seems surprised to see* **JANE** *still on the couch.*
>
> *Loathes her for even being there.*

JANE. *(Weak.)* Hi.

> **MARY ANNE** *ignores her, passive-aggressively starts to clean.*

How was your shift?

MARY ANNE. Fine.

> **MARY ANNE** *picks up the bottle of whiskey. She clocks the two glasses.*

JANE. We uh. I drank some of your whiskey but I'll replace it hope that's cool.

I didn't think you'd care 'cause I know you hate whiskey –

> **MARY ANNE** *goes to the sink, sees the dishes, sighs. Tosses the glasses in the sink.*

I'm gonna do those tonight.

> MARY ANNE *sighs aggressively.*
>
> *She takes the trash out of the trash can by herself. Closes it. It's hard.* JANE *watches* MARY ANNE *wrestle with the bag.*

JANE. I can do that –

> MARY ANNE *gives up. Breathes.*

MARY ANNE. It was Doug's whiskey.

JANE. ...Doug.

MARY ANNE. My ex-boyfriend. Remember?

Turns out he was sleeping with my friend? "Fun Stacey"? He moved out.

And you moved in.

> MARY ANNE *moves to the dishes, starts to wash them violently.*

JANE. I'm gonna do those for real – I wish you / wouldn't –

> *Violently,* MARY ANNE *throws a dish onto the floor. She stops. She breathes.*

MARY ANNE. *(Soft.)* I hate you.

JANE. What?

MARY ANNE. I HATE YOU.

You smell like PARMESAN CHEESE.

I work hard all day, I come home, I want *home*, I want QUIET, and there you are, sitting there all day, doing nothing.

JANE. *(Meek.)* Sometimes I do / things.

MARY ANNE. YOU ARE NOT CUTE. You suck. You make me SICK. I RUN A NINE-MINUTE MILE. And you sit around with my futon up your ass, watching my TV, that I NEVER get to watch, I pay for it, if you really WANTED a job you would GET a job, I haven't had a day off in two MONTHS and you are LAZY and I GET UP AT FIVE A.M., and you are PATHETIC.

> *She stops, breathes hard. Both are stunned.*

I am very tired.

> *Quietly,* **MARY ANNE** *dries her hands. She exits quickly toward her room. The door shuts.*
>
> **JANE** *stands up. She moves toward the dishes. She stares at them, unable to make herself do them.*

GAME. You have reached the bottom. You may:

> One: Continue on the trail.
>
> Two: Continue on the trail.
>
> Three: Continue on the trail.
>
> Four: Continue on the trail.

JANE. I'm done.

GAME. THAT IS NOT AN OPTION.

> PLEASE SELECT A VALID OPTION.

JANE. I don't wanna play anymore.

GAME. PLEASE SELECT AN OPTION AND PRESS SPACE BAR TO CONTINUE.

JANE. *(Helpless, defeated.)* I don't wanna / play anymore –

GAME. CONTINUING ON THE TRAIL.

> **JANE** *picks up the bottle of whiskey.*
>
> *She takes a deep sip.*
>
> *She pauses, winces.*

CONTINUING ON THE TRAIL.

> *She takes another.*

CONTINUING ON THE TRAIL.

> *She then takes another, pulling on it hard.*
>
> *She gags. Tears in her eyes.*
>
> *It's scary and real.*
>
> *Back on the trail,* **THEN JANE** *returns with an apron full of berries.*

THEN JANE. Sorry, sorry, I strayed off, got lost, I got some –

> *She spots* **CLANCY** *lying by the dying fire in pools of his own puke and shit.*

What –

CLANCY. Jane.

THEN JANE. I'll get some –

> *She grabs a jug of water, rushes over.*

CLANCY. Bad water, daughter –

THEN JANE. I still got some – from the stream –

> *She pours water from her water skin into* **CLANCY**'s *mouth.*

Pa, where's Mary Anne? I'll get Mary Anne.

CLANCY. She got it, too.

THEN JANE. *(Frantic.)* What should I do, Pa?

CLANCY. You gotta keep goin' –

THEN JANE. I can't, I can't –

CLANCY. You are strong, daughter – 's your nature –

THEN JANE. Not it's not, it's NOT – I can't go on alone, Pa! Don't make me go on alone!

> *Frantically she runs to the wagon, tearing around for medicine, grabbing blankets, anything. Helpless, alone.*
>
> *She fights back tears as she helplessly, worthlessly wraps them in blankets which they kick away, dying, writhing, expelling, puking.*
>
> *Back in the present,* **JANE** *pukes whiskey into the trash can.*
>
> *Reaches for more.*
>
> **MARY ANNE** *enters from her room, feeling sorry.*

MARY ANNE. I just –

> *She spots* **JANE** *chugging the whiskey, gagging.*

What're you doing?

> **JANE** *again throws up, then goes for more whiskey.*

STOP! Stop it –

> *MARY ANNE tries to take the whiskey from
> JANE, but JANE is fierce, fighting her off, trying
> to bring it again to her lips.*
>
> *Finally, MARY ANNE wrestles the bottle away
> from JANE.*
>
> *JANE heaves again into a trash can.*
>
> *She then lays there, writhing, expelling, as
> MARY ANNE processes what just happened.*

JANE. *(Groggy.)* Going forward in time – Forward – in
– time –

> *JANE considers this. Softly, she starts to cry.*
>
> *Back on the trail, helpless and alone, THEN
> JANE erupts.*

THEN JANE. HELPP!!
HELP ME PLEASE SOMEBODY HELP!!

JANE. *(Meek.)* ...Help.

> *She starts to cry.*

Help.

MARY ANNE. *(Determined.)* Okay.

> *Beat.*

Okay.

> *She strokes her sister's hair and thinks.*

PART IV

The trail.

THEN JANE *has finished burying* **MARY ANNE** *and* **CLANCY.**

She hefts large rocks to mark each grave.

She is exhausted from digging, from crying.

She lays at their feet and soundlessly weeps out all that's left inside of her.

Lights switch to include **JANE** *sitting on a stump in the same space.*

It's nighttime, on the top of a massive hill.

MARY ANNE *is arranging a sleeping bag.* **JANE** *watches her.*

GAME. Mount Pisgah, Oregon.

Weather: Sure.

Food: Two Luna bars.

Nearest Landmark: That Exxon before you head up the hill.

Morale: ...Nope.

Press space bar to continue.

JANE. *(Weary, defeated.)* Space bar.

> **MARY ANNE** *looks at her watch. She pulls a piece of paper out of her pocket, looks at it, begins to collect rocks.*

What is that, what're you doing?

MARY ANNE. I collected rocks for the healing circle you're going to make.

JANE. Nope. Don't want that.

MARY ANNE. You asked for help. This is me helping you.

JANE. So what do I do, do I just light myself on fire, or –

MARY ANNE. I looked up lots of different – first you write down all the things that're troubling you. Then you burn the clothes you've been wearing and with them, you burn the spirits of negativity that have been – like – clogging your – Yeah. Then there's some stuff with sage.

Handing to her.

Here's a print-out of the directions.

Handing again.

And here's the sage. It's a cleanse thing.

JANE. This is stupid.

MARY ANNE. *You're* stupid.

JANE. Do I have back-up clothes or do I sit here naked after?

> **MARY ANNE** *tosses her a backpack.*

MARY ANNE. Back-up.

> **MARY ANNE** *places the last rock and stands, gathering her things.*

JANE. You're leaving me here?

MARY ANNE. I have a night shift.

JANE. How'm I getting home?

MARY ANNE. I think you can handle it. Take a bus, figure it out.

JANE. What if I get murdered?

MARY ANNE. Maybe then you'll snap out of your whatever it is.

JANE. If I was MURDERED?

MARY ANNE. No one is going to murder you.

But here's some mace.

> *She hands it to her.*

JANE. Why're you being so mean to me?

MARY ANNE. Because somebody HAS TO BE.

> *Beat.*

The woman who brought her dead two-year-old into the ER last night after she accidentally ran over him with her second-hand minivan. SHE gets to not get out of bed. Not you. Mom and Dad won't say this to you, but I will. I can't live with you anymore like this.

And I know you don't have anywhere else to go.

So figure it out.

THEN JANE. But –

MARY ANNE. Just figure it out, Jane.

> **MARY ANNE** *goes.*

JANE. *(After her.)* This is not the answer!!

> *Frustrated, she settles into the dirt.*
>
> *A hawk cries. She jumps. She pulls the sleeping bag around her.*

GAME. May first. Mount Pisgah –

JANE. I KNOW WHERE I AM.

GAME. You may.

One: Continue on the trail.

Two: Learn about the trail.

Three: Learn about the trail.

Four: Learn about the trail.

Five: Learn about the trail.

JANE. OKAY. LEARN ABOUT THE TRAIL.

GAME. You will now learn about the trail.

> **JANE** *waits.*
>
> *Nothing happens.*

JANE. Great.

> *She reaches into her backpack, pulls out her Discman.*
>
> *Selects an old track,* tries to comfort herself with the nostalgia.*
>
> *She digs for her journal, starts to write.*

---

*A license to produce *The Oregon Trail* does not include a performance license for any third-party or copyrighted music. Licensees should create an original composition or use music in the public domain. For further information, please see Music Use Note on page 3.

My "troubles."

First trouble: my troubles are stupid and small.

I watch too much TV.

I can't decide whether or not I believe in God, and how there's no way to decide that but just decide that.

I am not beautiful or strong.

I will never be like my sister.

> *As* **JANE** *writes her list of troubles,* **THEN JANE** *returns with a fistful of wildflowers.*
>
> *She kneels by a makeshift grave and gently lays the flowers by each headstone.*
>
> *She isn't quite sure what to do with herself next.*
>
> *She then finds and digs through Clancy's satchel. Finds a knife.*
>
> *Considers it. The easy way out.*

I have no specificity or character.

> **THEN JANE** *sinks to the dust. Gives up. Gives in.*

THEN JANE. My family – is dead –

I don't know how to go on –

> **THEN JANE** *regards the knife in her hand.*

JANE. This is stupid.

> **JANE** *grabs her things, gets up to go. Trips over a rock. Falls.*
>
> *Curses the ground. Something catches her eye.*
>
> *She kneels down, takes a second look at what she tripped over.*
>
> *She moves grass aside.*
>
> *It's a small gravestone. Then Mary Anne's, long since grown over.*
>
> *She searches next to it, finds another – Clancy's.*

She is overcome with stillness, sadness.

A hawk cries.

Both **JANES** *look to the sky in terror.*

When they look down, they can see each other.

Just for a moment. Lights shift.

They stare at each other. Take each other in. It's a strange, suspended moment that will later in life be regarded as a vision or dream.

They sing together, a song that connects and opens and uplifts them, something like Aerosmith's "Amazing."*

The song ends. They stare at each other, linked.

THEN JANE *turns to dust and blows away in the wind.*

JANE *stands, renewed.*

Then:

Mary Anne's apartment, the next morning.

MARY ANNE *sits on the couch, numb from crying. Her violin sits next to her like an old friend she barely knows anymore.*

JANE. Mary Anne?

MARY ANNE *doesn't respond. She just shakes her head as tears start to come again.*

Are you crying?

MARY ANNE. No.

---

*A license to produce *The Oregon Trail* does not include a performance license for "Amazing." The publisher and author suggest that the licensee contact ASCAP or BMI to ascertain the music publisher and contact such music publisher to license or acquire permission for performance of the song. If a license or permission is unattainable for "Amazing," the licensee may not use the song in *The Oregon Trail* but should create an original composition in a similar style or use a similar song in the public domain. For further information, please see Music Use Note on page 3.

JANE. Yeah you are –

MARY ANNE. ...I got stuck on this elevator today. For like three hours. I didn't have my phone or anything. It was just me stuck in a very big box. I felt so powerless. And there was nothing else to do, except think and wait, and *think*. So much thinking. So slow. And so I started to make lists in my head to pass the time and then I started making lists of lists but then I ran out of lists and – and then I just – it started – I cried and I cried –

> *The tears come again.* **JANE** *puts a comforting hand on her sister's shoulder, or maybe pulls her fully into her arms, lets her cry.*

But it's all so stupid because I have a good job, I have a good life, everything's fine in the grand scheme of things, so why am I *so* – why do I feel so –

JANE. Sad?

Welcome to my world.

MARY ANNE. Your world sucks ass.

JANE. Yeah, it does.

MARY ANNE. I just feel...so...*why?* I'm just a person. I am just a tiny person and I – I get up every morning. I wash my face. I go to work. I come home. I go to sleep. I go to work. And I could just – stop. And would it even matter? Would anyone even – does anything I do even *matter?*

JANE. Yeah. It does.

MARY ANNE. Why?

JANE. Because you're alive.

MARY ANNE. ...Yeah. I guess.

JANE. Just like everybody who came before you. They were alive, and so – so are we.

> *Beat.*

Maybe when we feel this – the –

> *She still can't quite name it. Puts a hand on her gut.*

JANE. Maybe that's just our bodies remembering them.

>   *Beat.*

MARY ANNE. That's – that's so *sad* –

>   **MARY ANNE** *starts to cry. She can't help it.*

JANE. I KNOW!

MARY ANNE. Oh my God –

JANE. Right?!

MARY ANNE. THAT IS SO SAD!!

JANE. THANK YOU! I KNOW!

>   *Then, realizing:*

But also – it's not. Because it makes us remember where we came from. And where we're going. And why we're going there, at all.

MARY ANNE. ...Yeah. I guess so.

>   **JANE** *is now in tears too. Takes* **MARY ANNE***'s hand.*

>   **MARY ANNE** *dries her tears.*

JANE. I see you found your violin.

MARY ANNE. I was reorganizing my closet / and it –

JANE. Why were you reorganizing your closet?

MARY ANNE. Because I LIKE to, I LIKE to reorganize my closet, that is my idea of fun.

JANE. You're a crazy / person.

MARY ANNE. I know.

>   *Beat.*

I took it out to play it but I can't even play it anymore. I barely remember how.

JANE. Let's hear it.

MARY ANNE. No.

JANE. C'monnnnnn.

>   **MARY ANNE** *hesitates but then, sniffing, picks up the violin.*

>   *She plays "Skip to My Lou." She's terrible.*

As she plays we see **THEN JANE** *dragging her mother's rocking chair through the dust, determined, pushing on toward Oregon.*

MARY ANNE.
LOU LOU
SKIP TO MY LOU

> **JANE** *laughs, delighted.* **MARY ANNE** *is bad at something, and it is wonderful.*

LOU LOU
SKIP TO MY LOU
LOU LOU
SKIP TO MY LOU
SKIP TO MY LOU MY DARLING.

JANE. Wow. Who sucks now?

MARY ANNE. Shut up!

JANE. It's you!

MARY ANNE. I know!

> **MARY ANNE** *keeps playing through her laughter.*
>
> *As she does, back on the trail,* **THEN JANE** *spots something in the distance. Something familiar, heaven-like, warm and welcoming. She picks up her pace, exhausted, overjoyed, and moves toward it.*

LOU LOU
SKIP TO MY LOU
LOU LOU
SKIP TO MY LOU
LOU LOU
SKIP TO MY LOU
SKIP TO MY LOU MY DARLING.

GAME. CONGRATULATIONS. You have made it to Oregon.

> *The* **JANES** *smile.*

End of Play